Where does it go?

WHERE DOES IT GO?
2024
Text © Erin Whitlatch
Illustration and Design © Felipe Matos
All rights reserved.

ISBN 9798306241678

written by **Erin Whitlatch**

illustrated by **Felipe Matos**

Where does it go?

For my curious daughter, Juliette
- E.W.

Wake up, get dressed and look outside,
"the garbage truck is coming!" Juju cried.

Down the stairs at the day's first glow,
Juju wonders "where does the trash go?"

The truck stops at every house until it moves all the trash into the landfill.

Machines will crush the trash then stop,
and soil will then be poured on top.

Across the road, a school bus bright yellow,
doors open and the driver waves hello.

Kids climb up the steps to find a seat,
then the bus moves on further down the street.

It turns the corner nice and slow,
Juju wonders "where will the bus go?"

Buses drive lots of children to school
where they'll listen and learn and follow the rules.

There are classrooms and lunch time and at recess kids play,
then the bus brings them home at the end of the day.

Up in the sky, next to a cloud,
an airplane is flying so fast and loud.

Juju stands tall as if she's trying to grow,
then asks, "but now where will that plane go?"

Planes can be going to all sorts of places.
They fit many people and all their suitcases.

On trips or vacations or even homebound,
planes are the fastest way to travel around.

From the backseat of the car, Juju hears the siren.
It gets closer and louder, then she sees the firemen.

The firetruck passes, lights flashing and glowing,
Juju wonders out loud "mom, where are they going?"

Firetrucks respond to all kinds of requests to
put out fires or perform a rescue.
Down the street, horns blasting, you may see them speed,
they are fast on their way to help people in need.

Spring, summer and fall, we count the birds soaring, dipping and diving and up high exploring.

Then weather turns cold and we start to see snow,
Juju asks, "where did all the birds go?"

Not all birds like snow and will fly south where it's warm.
They live there through the winter and skip the snowstorms.

In the spring when it's finally warm, that is when, they will fly back and you will see them again.

Juju thought about all that she learned,

knowledge of all these new things that she earned...

She sat down with mom, and said with a sigh...

"You've told me where, now can you tell me WHY?"

Made in the USA
Monee, IL
17 April 2025

15941035R00021